ANNUAL 2024

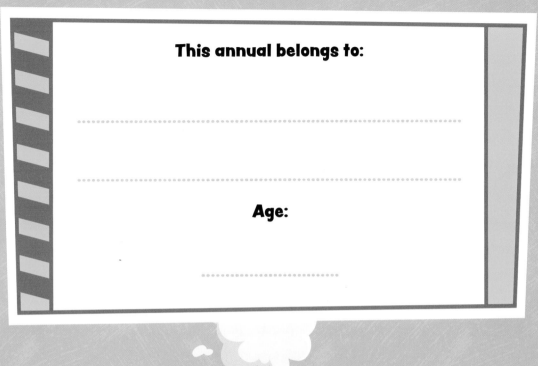

This annual belongs to:

....

....

Age:

....

ANNUAL 2024

Farshore

THOMAS
1
#1 ENGINE!

PERCY
6
CHOO-HOO!

First published in Great Britain in 2023 by Farshore
An imprint of HarperCollins*Publisher*s
1 London Bridge Street, London SE1 9GF
www.farshore.co.uk

HarperCollins*Publishers*
Macken House, 39/40 Mayor Street Upper, Dublin 1, D01 C9W8, Ireland

Written by Laura Jackson.

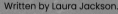

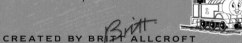

HiT entertainment

CREATED BY BRITT ALLCROFT

Based on The Railway Series by The Reverend W Awdry.
©2023 Gullane (Thomas) Limited. Thomas the Tank Engine & Friends™
and Thomas & Friends™ are trademarks of Gullane (Thomas) Limited.
©2023 HIT Entertainment Limited. HIT and the HIT logo are
trademarks of HIT Entertainment Limited.

ISBN 978 0 00 853716 6
Printed in Romania
001

A CIP catalogue record for this title is available from the British Library.

Parental guidance is advised for all craft and colouring activities.
Always ask an adult to help when using glue, paint and scissors.
Wear protective clothing and cover surfaces to avoid staining.

Stay safe online.
Farshore is not responsible for content hosted by third parties.

Farshore takes its responsibility to the planet and its inhabitants
very seriously. We aim to use papers from well-managed forests
run by responsible suppliers.

KANA
THAT'S ELECTRIC!

NIA
18
ABSO-TOOT-LEY!

DIESEL
AW, BOLTS!

BRUNO
43
BRAKES ON!

Contents

Meet the Sodor Squad
Chugga-chugga-woo-hoo!
Team Awesome is coming through! Hop on board to meet the buddies for some speedy fun.

Hello, Thomas
The number 1 engine is ready to take you on some loop-the-loop adventures.

Hello, Kana
Hold on tight, the fastest engine on Sodor is about to go for a bumpity-bumpity ride!

Hello, Diesel
Here comes Diesel, looking for fun ... and maybe some mischief too!

Hello, Percy
All aboard the mail train! Percy is ready to giggle his merry way through Sodor.

Hello, Bruno
I don't want to put the brakes on the fun, let's go!

Hello, Nia!
Watch out for a whoosh of colour whizzing down the tracks. Let the adventures begin!

Let's Rock and Roll

Thomas wants to play at Lookout Mountain, but there is lots to do along the way. Follow the wibbly-wobbly tracks with your finger and help Thomas with his challenges.

Let's go!

Count up the hot-air balloons.

I can count [ ] hot-air balloons.

Baaa! Five sheep have escaped. **Circle them!**

START

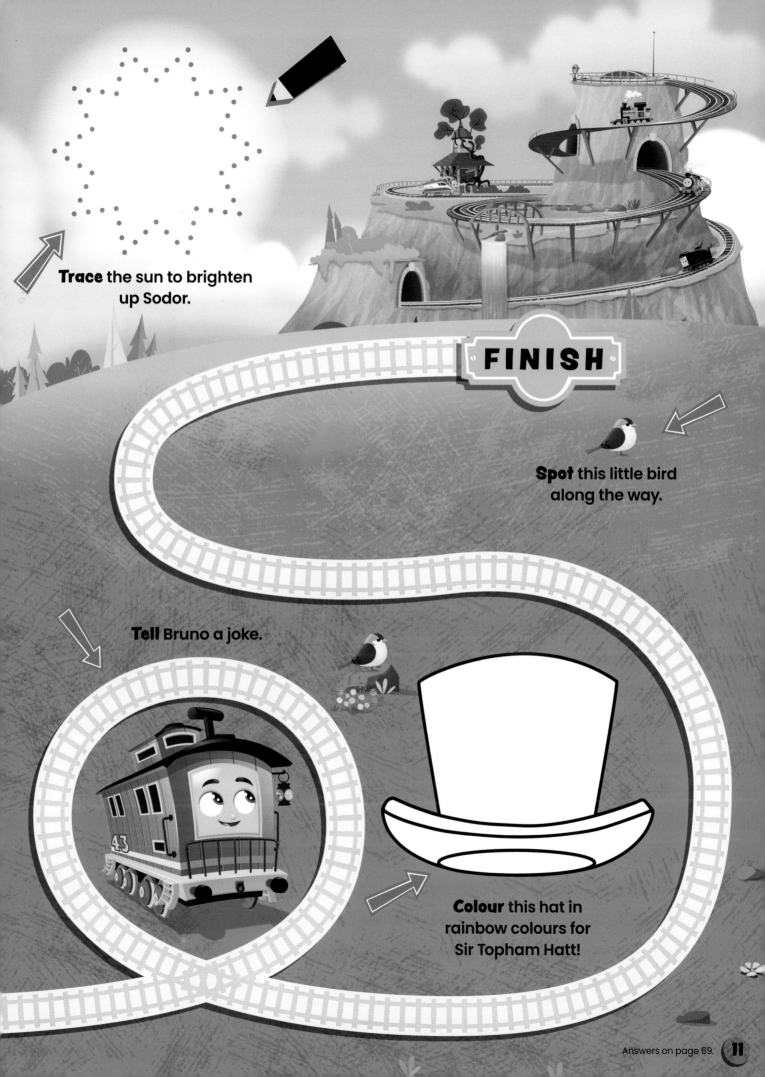

Trace the sun to brighten up Sodor.

FINISH

Spot this little bird along the way.

Tell Bruno a joke.

Colour this hat in rainbow colours for Sir Topham Hatt!

Go, Go Thomas

Fast, friendly and fun, Thomas is always ready for new adventures and meeting new friends.
No mission is too big or small for this little engine!

THOMAS FACTS

Thomas is: cheeky but always kind

Colour: blue

Likes: doing loop-the-loops!

Fun fact: Percy is Thomas' best friend

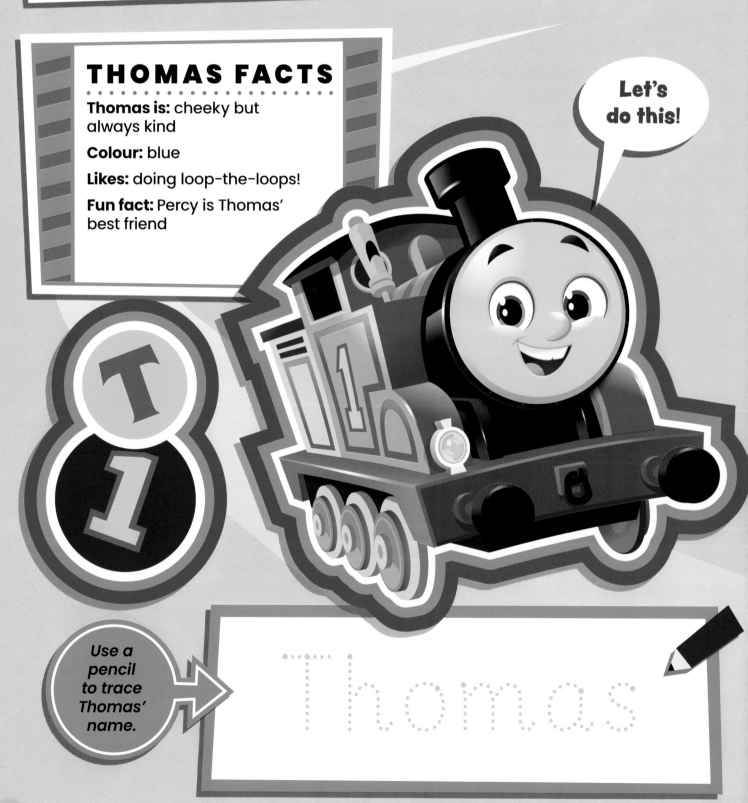

Let's do this!

Use a pencil to trace Thomas' name.

Thomas

Animal Antics

Thomas loves meeting all the animals on Sodor. They are so funny!

Help Thomas count up the pigs, then the sheep and then the noisy cows. **Mooooo!**

Use the number line to point to your answers.

Answers on page 69.

Hide and Surprise

On the Island of Sodor, the sun was shining and it was the perfect day for a game of **Hide and Surprise**. Only Diesel wasn't happy, because he was losing.

Every time he found a hiding space, Percy would find him.

Behind the haystack,

in front of a bush,

even behind a carriage.

Percy found Diesel wherever he hid. **"Slippery slip switch!"** grumbled Diesel.

For the next round, Diesel was determined to find the **best hiding spot** on the island. He jumped onto a barge at Brendam Docks and hid between some crates.

"Hee-hee, Percy will never find me here!" he giggled.

Little did he know, he had accidentally loosened the barge ropes. The barge was now floating out of the docks!

When Diesel peeped around the crates to see where Percy was, he was surprised to see he was bobbing up and down in the middle of the sea.

"**Rusty rail spikes!**" Diesel cried out.

Meanwhile, Percy had been **looking everywhere** for Diesel and Thomas was helping too.

Cranky noticed that one barge was missing, and he quickly told Percy and Thomas.

"So ... Diesel might be hiding on the missing barge!" gasped Percy. "**We've got to find him.**"

Poor Diesel could see his friends from way out at sea, but they couldn't see him.

"I'm finally winning at Hide and Surprise, but I just want to get back on land," Diesel told a passing seagull.

Poor Diesel tried his hardest to get back to the docks, but it was no use. He just couldn't stretch or jump far enough to make it safely onto land.

He even tried to flap up and down like a seagull, but he only made a dusty mess.

"**Nuts and bolts**!" said Diesel. "I'm in big trouble."

Diesel suddenly felt very silly for taking the game so seriously.

Lucky for Diesel, his friends were not about to give up on him.

Whirr! Whirr! Whirr! High up in the sky, Harold **whooshed** over the floating barge.

"Ahoy there, Diesel!" Harold shouted down. "I hear you could do with some help!"

Harold threw down a rope and heaved and pulled and heaved and pulled. But the barge was heavy, and the rope went **SNAP!**

"I'm going to be on this barge forever," said Diesel. "I miss my friends."

When Diesel had almost given up hope, he noticed something in the distance. It was Bulstrode, with Percy and Thomas on board.

"**Found you!**" giggled Percy, as they rescued a very grateful Diesel.

When they were safely back at the docks, Diesel was very happy to be on dry land again.

"We're glad we found you," said Percy. "Your hiding place really was a surprise."

"And I have never been so happy to lose at Hide and Surprise," giggled Diesel.

Found You!

Shhh ... Thomas is playing Hide and Surprise.
His friends have found some top-secret hiding places.
Draw lines to match up who is hiding where.

Shout out **'Found you!'** *each time you find a friend.*

a

b

c

d

Players:

Nia

Diesel

Percy

Sandy

Sandy to the Rescue

Yucky mucky! Thomas is stuck in the mud.
Help Sandy choose the right track to help her friend.
Watch out for tracks that lead to more mushy mud.

Let's work together!

1
2
3

Now colour in this special badge – just for you!

I helped the Sodor Squad!

Go, Go Percy

Percy is a happy little engine and is always by Thomas' side. He sometimes gets scared of the dark, monsters and ghosts ... but he faces his fears head on!

PERCY FACTS

Percy is: gentle but loves to joke around

Colour: green

Likes: having adventures with Thomas

Fun fact: he rings his lucky bell if he needs good luck

Let's rock and roll!

6

Use a pencil to trace Percy's name.

Percy

Copy Colour

Whee! Here comes Percy!
Use the little picture to help
you colour in the big picture.

Christmas Dash

It's Thomas against Nia in a **wibbly-wobbly** Christmas race. Follow the tracks to find out who collects the most decorations along the way.

Thomas

Nia

Colour in a present for Thomas and Nia to say well done for taking part.

Fast Friends

Carly and Sandy are best friends.
When they work together, they can do anything.
Draw a line to link up the matching pair of pictures.

Tyrannosaurus Wrecks

Deep underground, in the dusty, rusty mine, the engines were busy hunting for treasure.

Over the bump and round the bend, Diesel had spotted something **HUGE** ...

"**M-m-monster!**" he cried out.

Sandy rolled up to the friends. "It's not a monster, it's a dinosaur!" she giggled.

Diesel had discovered the best treasure of all – the bones of a Tyrannosaurus Rex.

"**Cool!**" said Thomas.

And what was even cooler was that the engines were allowed to take the bones to Vicarstown Museum for a dinosaur show.

In no time at all, the heavy bones were split up and ready for delivery.

"Everybody, pick a car of bones," Gordon told the engines. "But keep them in the exact order they are in now."

The dinosaur was going to be put back together again at the museum. If the engines got mixed up, T. rex might get jumbled up too.

"Let's **dino-ROAR!**" said Thomas.

The engines sang as they whizzed across Sodor, being very careful to stay in order:

"Feet, tailbone, ribs and claws, head and jaws.

Feet, tailbone, ribs and claws, head and jaws!"

Soon the museum was in sight. The last downhill track meant one thing ... a roaring race to the finish.

Whoosh!

"*Diesel-ceratops* knows the shortcuts!" shouted out Diesel.

But now the engines were racing each other, nobody was in the right order anymore.

Speedy Kana skidded up to Sandy and Carly at the museum in first place.

"Hey, *Train-osauruses*," said Carly. "Are your bones first, Kana?"

Kana wasn't so sure. "Erm, maybe ..." she frowned.

Whirr, clank, bang! Sandy and Carly worked hard to put T. rex back together again.

Only, T. rex didn't look like T. rex anymore. All the bones were the wrong way around!

No matter how many times Carly and Sandy tried to fix it, T. rex was still jumbled up.

"Now it's an *upside-downosaurus*," sighed Sandy.

The engines' race had messed up the order of the bones. All the engines felt terrible for not listening to Gordon.

Diesel was not ready to give up. He tried with all his might to remember what T. rex had looked like on the mine wall.

But even with Diesel's super-duper memory, T. rex looked worse than ever. It was nearly time for the dinosaur show, and there was no dinosaur to show.

Suddenly the rails rumbled and shook as Gordon arrived.

"I told you to stay in order," he said crossly, but he wanted to help. "Just think back to how you were lined up in the first place ..." he added.

"The song!" puffed Nia. "We need to remember the song to remember the order."

The engines sang loudly: *"Feet, tailbone, ribs and claws, head and jaws.*   *"Feet, tailbone, ribs and claws, head and jaws!"*

This time, Sandy and Carly knew exactly what to do. There was not a jumbled-up bone in sight. T. rex looked totally roar-some!

"Hang on!" shouted out Diesel. "We have forgotten a bone."

There was one big bone left over. But it wasn't a T. rex bone.

"That's a tusk for a woolly mammoth," gasped Sandy.

"Sounds like a new job for ... **the Biggest Adventure Club!**" peeped Thomas.

"Feet, tailbone, ribs and claws, head and jaws ... and TUSK!"

ROAR!

Go, Go Kana

Fizzing, whizzing Kana is an electric super speeder.
The rails **rock and roll** when she is at top speed. **Whoosh!**

KANA FACTS

Kana is: fast, fun and always ready to roll

Colour: purple

Likes: racing her friends – and winning!

Fun fact: Kana is from Japan

That's electric!

Use a pencil to trace Kana's name.

Kana

Kind Kana

Percy is scared of the dark, and he is lost in the night. Quickly guide Kana through Sodor to rescue her friend.

Follow ONLY the **stars** ★ and **moons** ☾ to find Percy.

Bubble Trouble

It's fun getting muddy, but it is super fun getting bubbly clean. Guide Diesel through the washdown so he can be the first engine to get clean.

Stay away from muddy friends!

START

FINISH

Use a black crayon to make Diesel shiny again.

Everybody's Welcome

Sodor is a place for everyone.
Tall, small, fast, slow, loud, quiet, red, blue ...
Sir Topham Hatt welcomes everybody.

Can you take his special Sodor quiz?

1 Circle the **smallest** friend.

a   b   c   d

2 Circle the **tallest** friend.

a   b   c   d

3 Circle the **fluffiest** friend.

a   b   c   d

4 Circle the **fastest** friend.

a   b   c   d

Terrific Thomas

Join the black dots to make a fun picture of the number 1 engine. Then use the coloured spots to help you colour in your picture.

By ....

write name here

Team Awesome

Thomas and Kana are helping care for the environment. Draw **X**s on the items of rubbish and recycling that they should collect.

Paper, card, plastic, tin cans and glass can be recycled into new things, so they can be used again.

Go, Go Bruno

Bruno is an autistic Brake Car who loves routines and being on time. He flashes his lanterns and flaps his stairs to let his friends know he is feeling excited or upset.

BRUNO FACTS

Bruno is: helpful and keeps heavy deliveries steady and on track

Colour: red

Likes: being on time, every time

Fun fact: he often rolls in reverse, so he gets a fun view of Sodor

Toot-ally on time!

43

Use a pencil to trace Bruno's name.

Bruno

A Perfect Plan

When Bruno rolls in reverse, he gets to see so much more of Sodor. Help Bruno keep to his schedule by **zooming** past his friends in this order:

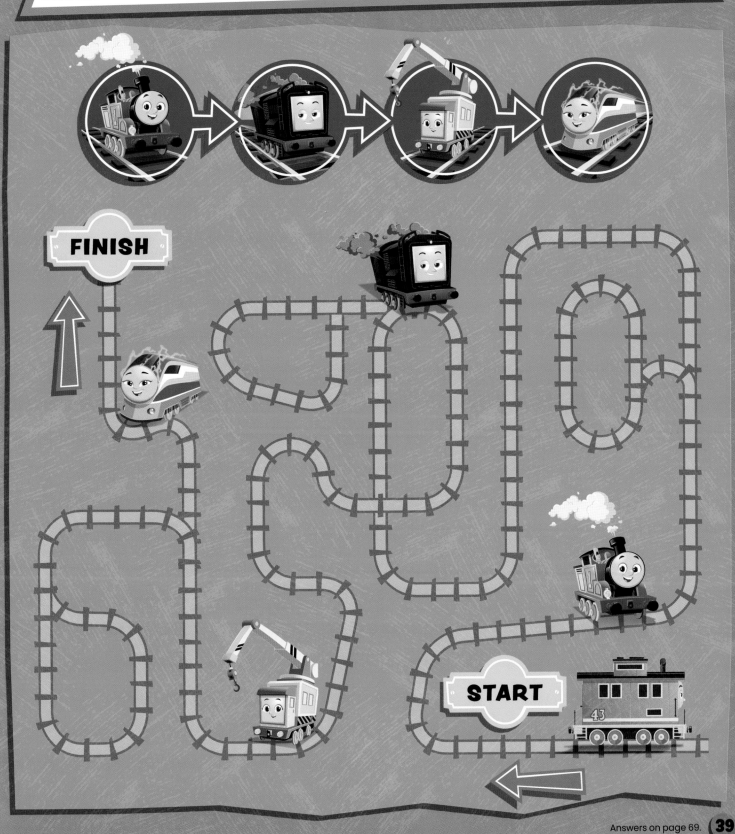

FINISH

START

Happy Birthday, Kana

It's Kana's birthday and Sir Topham Hatt
has organised a rocking party for her.
Even T. rex has dressed up!

Can you spot ...?

*Shout out
Happy birthday!
each time you
spot one.*

Biggest Adventure Club

It was an exciting day on the Island of Sodor. Thomas had found a map in the water tower. And it wasn't just any old map.

"Thomas, you have found the map to the **Crystal Cave**," puffed Gordon, in surprise.

The engines had all heard stories about the mysterious Crystal Cave. It was said to be filled with crystals of every colour and home to a sparkling crystal train.

"Some people don't believe it exists," said Percy. He stared at the map. "Look, it says the cave is in the old mine."

Thomas couldn't wait to find out more. "This is a job for the **Big Adventure Club!**" he said.

Sandy wanted to join the club too, but the other engines weren't so sure.

"The mine is dark and scary ..." said Percy.

"You're a bit little for this adventure," said Thomas, gently.

"Humph!" Sandy didn't feel little, and she never got scared.

She steamed off to find Diesel. When he heard about the Big Adventure Club, he was cross to be left out too.

"Let's start our own **Bigger Adventure Club**," said Sandy. "Then we can find the cave before them."

"Sparking idea!" grinned Diesel.

Meanwhile, the Big Adventure Club was ready to roll. Percy had stocked up on gadgets, lights and a ... snorkel.

"An adventurer should be prepared for anything," said Percy, proudly.

But Percy didn't feel brave for long. Inside the mine, it was dark and super spooky.

The engines **bumpity-bumped** along the rickety rollercoaster rails. There were so many bumps and bends, the friends were soon completely lost.

"Maybe I should have joined the Littlest Adventure Club instead," whispered Percy.

Sandy and Diesel were having better luck. They had already spotted sparkles in the mine walls.

"Crystals ..." gasped Sandy. "The Bigger Adventure Club is on the right track!"

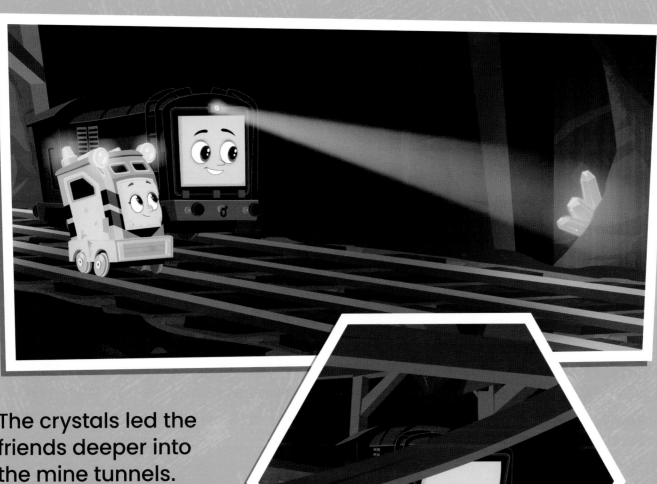

The crystals led the friends deeper into the mine tunnels. The tunnels got smaller and smaller, until Diesel couldn't go any further. He was too big.

"Wait!" he called out.

The **twisty tunnels** were no problem for little Sandy. She had already zipped off, all on her own.

Oh no! thought Diesel. Sandy would be very scared without him.

Back through the tunnels, Diesel nearly crashed into The Big Adventure Club. Thomas, Percy and Carly were zooming around in circles, still completely lost.

"Get us out of here!" said Percy.

Suddenly, Sandy's voice echoed in the distance. "**Woohooo! Woohoo!**"

"Sandy's lost too?" asked Percy. "She must be really scared on her own."

But Sandy wasn't scared at all. She had found the Crystal Cave, all by herself!

"**Epic!**" shouted Sandy.

Everywhere she looked, giant rainbow crystals sparkled in the light. It was beautiful.

Sandy's excited voice led the engines all the way to the cave. The crystal train sparkled above the engines.

"**Woah!**" the friends cried.

"I'm sorry I said you were too little, Sandy," blushed Thomas. "You are definitely big enough ..."

"And brave enough," giggled Percy.

"Let's start a new club, for all of us," said Thomas. "the **Biggest Adventure Club!**"

"And for our first adventure," said Percy. "Let's find our way out of here!"

Story Quiz

How much can you remember about the **Biggest Adventure Club?** Read the story on page 42 then take this quiz about it.

1

What did Thomas find in the old water tower?

a a sheep

b a map

c a crystal

2

Who did Sandy ask to be in her Bigger Adventure Club?

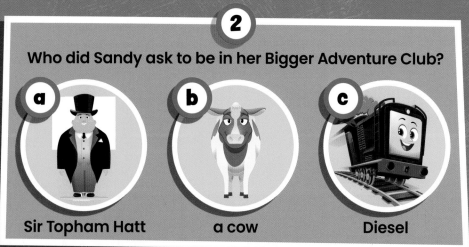

a Sir Topham Hatt

b a cow

c Diesel

3

Where was the Crystal Cave?

a the old mine

b Lookout Mountain

c Cannonball Curve

4

What was inside the Crystal Cave?

a rainbows

b a crystal train

c birds

Now go back to the story and see how many questions you got right.

Which Thomas?

Thomas has lots of different feelings. He can feel happy, sad, cross, excited, bored, worried, determined ... all in one day!

Can you find these three faces hiding below?

 excited

 determined

 worried

What feelings have you felt today?

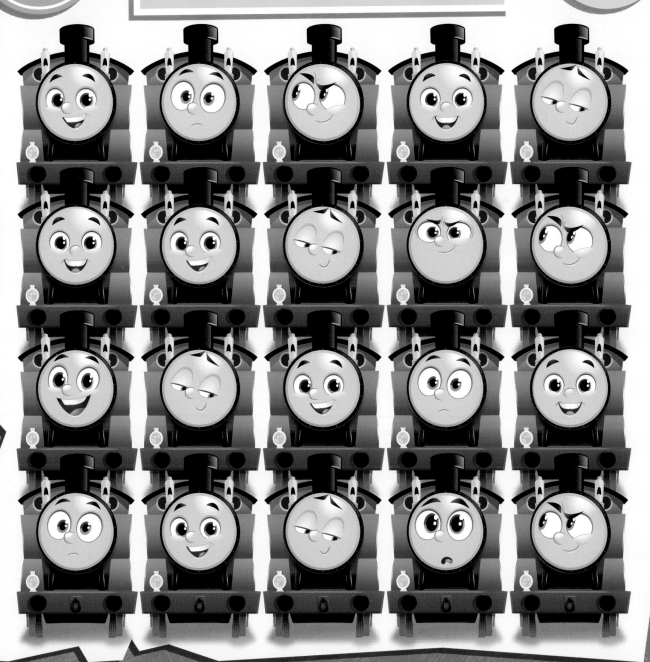

Funny Close-ups

Percy, Bruno, Thomas and Diesel are wearing disguises today. Don't they look funny!
Can you spot the small close-ups in the big picture?

Colour Splash

It's time for a new paint job, but the paint pots are all mixed up. Draw lines to match the right colour splat to each friend.

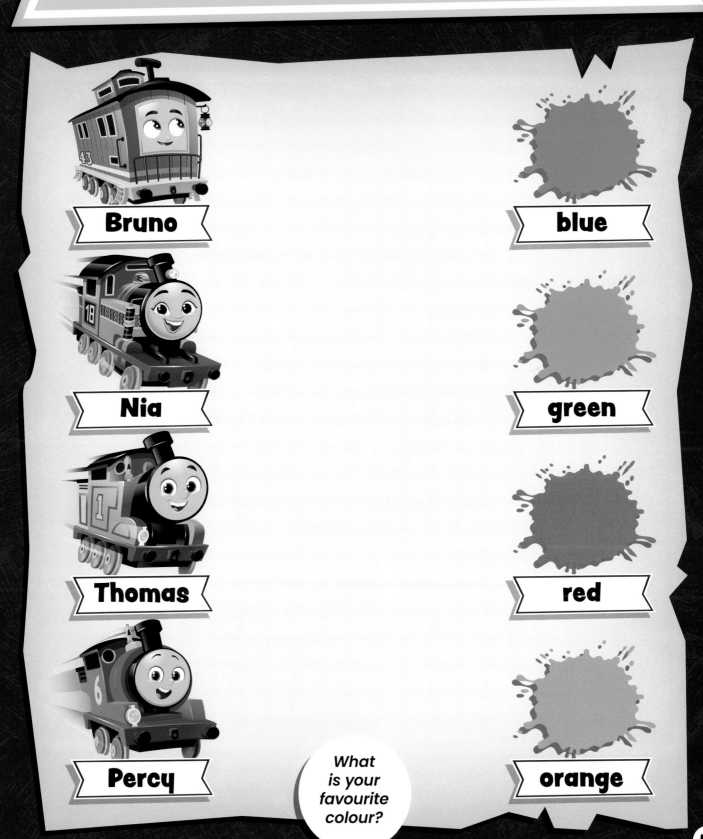

Bruno

Nia

Thomas

Percy

blue

green

red

orange

What is your favourite colour?

Sparkly Spot

All the friends are ready for a sparkle-tastic, jumpy-bumpy adventure in the Crystal Cave. Can you find 5 differences in picture 2?

Colour in a crystal each time you spot one.

Twisty Tracks

Grab a pencil and follow the engines' **tracks!**

Wind round the bends **with Thomas!**

Go round in a circle **with Percy!**

Speed down the line **with Kana!**

Loop-the-loop **with Harold!**

Zig and zag **with Diesel!**

Go, Go Nia

Nia brightens up the tracks wherever she goes. From Africa to Sodor, she has travelled the world and loves to share adventures with her best friends.

NIA FACTS

Nia is: colourful, kind and clever

Colour: orange, red, yellow, purple and green

Likes: listening to music and singing

Fun fact: Nia is from Kenya in Africa

Let the adventure begin!

18

Use a pencil to trace Nia's name.

Nia

Catch Me If You Can

Whoosh! Kana and Nia are fast friends – they love to play and race together. Can you spot the odd one out before they **whizz** away?

Answers on page 69.

Wild Weather

Sodor adventures are fun in the rain, sun, snow and wind. Draw lines to match the correct type of weather to each picture.

1  snow

2  rain

3  sun

4  wind

a

b

c

d

Racing Rainbows

Wow! Thomas and Percy have found a big rainbow in the sky. Colour it in bright colours to make the friends super happy.

Did you know? A rainbow appears when sunlight shines through rain.

Overnight Stop

Read all about Percy's big night out.
Say the words out loud when you see the pictures.

Percy  **Thomas**  **Nia**  **stars**  **bell**  **light**

, and  were asleep in their cosy sheds. But it was time to get up! The engines had to go on an overnight delivery.

"But where will we sleep?" asked .

"We can camp under the in the woods!" peeped .

liked sleeping inside, with his night and his cloud picture. Sleeping outside sounded scary.

 didn't dare to tell how scared he was feeling. Instead, he rang his lucky to bring him good luck and loaded a truck with things to help him sleep. But, poor ! During the long journey, his truck rolled away.

When the friends arrived at the woods, realised his bedtime supplies were gone. His lucky hadn't worked! He felt very scared, and this time, he told and exactly how he was feeling.

"It's OK to be nervous," said , kindly.

"Camping under the can be scary, but fun too!"  and had an idea. They would bring home to ! They found three trees like their sheds, puffed some steam to make a cloud picture and used Nia's for a night.

Now didn't feel scared at all. He looked up at the and felt like he was home. Brave Percy!

Night, night!

What makes you feel scared?

I'M THE

 # 1

ENGINE

Spooky Shadows

Oooooooh! It's spooky in the dark mine today.
Draw lines to match each shadow to the friend.

1

2

3

4

5

a

b

c

d

e

Answers on page 69.

Bruno's Big Challenge

Bruno knows all the schedules and routes. He can't wait to see his friends around Sodor. Try doing his Big Challenge – there's lots of fun things for you to do today!

HOW TO PLAY

- Choose an engine and try your best to do the challenge.
- If it's a bit hard, just choose another engine!
- Colour in the star when you complete each task.
- How many challenges can you do?

Gordon
Be helpful at home and tidy all your toys away.

Nia
Go outside and play today.

Thomas
Do a funny dance to make somebody giggle!

Percy
Draw a picture for somebody in your home.

Sandy
Look at the sky. Can you see any shapes in the clouds?

Carly
Sing your favourite song out loud.

Kana
Help a grown-up make a healthy meal.

Bruno
Have some quiet time and read a book.

Diesel
Play hide-and-seek with somebody in your family.

You did it! You are a star!

....
write name here

completed Bruno's Big Challenge

67

Better Together

No two friends on Sodor are the same.
It's their differences that make them all special.

Use crayons to colour these posters in your own super style.

Answers

Page 10 Let's Rock and Roll
There are six hot-air balloons.

Page 13 Animal Antics
There are 4 cows, 5 sheep and 8 pigs.

Page 20 Found You!
a.   Percy
b.   Nia
c.   Sandy
d.   Diesel

Page 21 Sandy to the Rescue
Track 1 leads to Thomas.

Page 24 Christmas Dash
Thomas collected 5.
Nia collected 6.

Page 25 Fast Friends
1 and 6 are a matching pair.

Page 33 Kind Kana

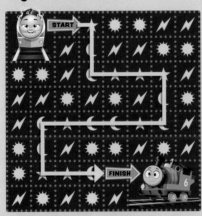

Page 34 Bubble Trouble

Page 35 Everybody's Welcome
1 = c, 2 = b, 3 = c, 4 = b

Page 37 Team Awesome

Page 39 A Perfect Plan

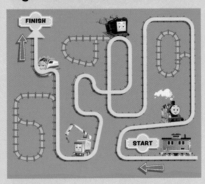

**Pages 40–41
Happy Birthday, Kana**

Page 48 Story Quiz
1 = b, 2 = c, 3 = a, 4 = b

Page 49 Which Thomas?

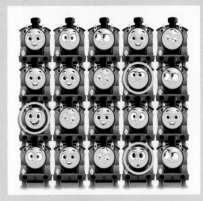

Page 50 Funny Close-ups

Page 51 Colour Splash
Bruno is red, Nia is orange, Thomas is blue and Percy is green.

Pages 52-53 Sparkly Spot

Page 57 Catch Me if You Can
3 is the odd one out.

Page 58 Wild Weather
1 = c, 2 = d, 3 = a, 4 = b

Page 65 Spooky Shadows
1 = e, 2 = c, 3 = a, 4 = b, 5 = d